Brock Cole

BUTTONS

A SUNBURST BOOK · FARRAR, STRAUS AND GIROUX

For Frances and Andrew

Distributed in Canada by Douglas & McIntyre Ltd.

Printed in the United States of America

First edition, 2000

Sunburst edition, 2004

1   3   5   7   9   10   8   6   4   2

Library of Congress Cataloging-in-Publication Data

Cole, Brock.

   Buttons / Brock Cole.

      p.   cm.

      Summary: When their father eats so much that he pops the buttons off his
britches, each of his three daughters tries a different plan to find replacements.

      ISBN 0-374-41013-5 (pbk.)

      [1. Fathers and daughters—Fiction.   2. Humorous stories.]   I. Title.

PZ7.C67342Bu 2000

                                                                                    99-27162

Once there was an old man who ate so much his britches burst and his buttons popped one, two, three, into the fire.

"Wife! Wife!" he cried. "We are undone! My britches have burst and my buttons are burnt, every one!"

His wife helped him to bed and then went to find their three daughters.

"Children," she said. "A terrible thing has happened. Your father has burst his britches and his buttons are burnt, front and back, every one. What are we to do?"
The three girls rolled their eyes at the ceiling and thought and thought.

The eldest—a slender beauty—spoke first. "I know not what course my sisters may choose," she said, "but I shall dress in my finest clothes and walk up and down the Palace Bridge. Surely a rich man will fall in love with me and ask me to be his wife. But I will say, 'No! I can never be yours! Not unless you first give me all of your buttons!'"

"An excellent plan!" cried her mother. "Come to my arms, my precious child."

Then the second daughter spoke up. She was tall and strong and had bright red cheeks. "Mother," she said, "I don't know what little sister will do, but I shall dress as a boy and join the army. Surely you have noticed that a soldier's uniform has many, many buttons. I have no doubt I shall be able to spare two or three for Father."

"What a splendid idea! Let me embrace you as well, my darling girl!" cried her mother and then waited expectantly to hear what her youngest daughter might suggest.

Well! This girl couldn't think of a thing. She was young and rabbity and still picked her nose when she thought no one was looking. How could she come up with a plan as wonderful as those of her sisters?

Still, she screwed up her eyes and twisted her fingers until they hurt.

"I know what I shall do," she said finally. "I will run in the meadows along the river, and I will hold my apron out so that if any buttons should fall from the sky, I will catch them before they get lost in the tall grass."

"Very good!" said her mother and gave her a pat. Privately the old woman had her doubts, but since the older girls had such marvelous ideas, it hardly seemed to matter what the youngest did.

And so the eldest daughter dressed up in her finest robe and jewels, and the second put on a boy's rough jacket and leather britches, and the youngest left off her shoes and stockings to run in the meadows along the river.

And now we shall hear what happened to them all.

The eldest daughter had not walked to and fro upon the bridge for twenty minutes when suddenly a band of ruffians set upon her. They tore her gown and stole her purse and tipped her over the balustrade so that she fell headfirst down, down, down into the river below.

It might have been all up with her, but a handsome young bargee pulled her from the water just as she was about to drown. When he saw how beautiful she was, even with duckweed in her hair and her clothes all torn, he fell in love at once.

"Will you be my wife?" he said. "I'm going on a long voyage through many countries to my home in Cologne and must have you by my side or expire of a broken heart. Please say you'll be mine."

"All right," said the eldest sister. It seemed only decent under the circumstances.

She and the bargee were married at once by the captain of a passing sightseeing boat, and in no time at all were on their way down the river. The eldest daughter was very happy with her new husband, and it was only when they were in sight of Cologne's cathedral spires that she remembered that she had married him without demanding a single button. No, not even something niggly made of bone.

Oh, bother, she thought, but what's done is done, and can't be undone. She decided she would send her father a postcard instead.

The second sister joined the army, just as she had resolved. But no sooner had she put on her fine uniform with sixty gold buttons up and down the front and at the sleeves and on her trousers and puttees than there came a report that their country was besieged! Her regiment was ordered to the front at once!

What a battle there was! Cannons roared and sabers clashed. Musket shot hummed through the air like a million angry bees. Was it the brave young ensign falling senseless from his horse? Yes, it was!

The second sister caught the ensign in her strong arms and carried him to the safety of a nearby cowshed. He was wounded. A flesh wound only, but it bled profusely. At once the girl tore off her jacket and made bandages from her shirttails. Many buttons were lost and destroyed in the process, but who could think of buttons at a time like this?

When the young ensign came to his senses, the first thing he saw was a golden-haired young woman bending over him, her eyes filled with concern. What goddess is this, he thought, that holds me in her arms? Surely I have died and gone to paradise. But no, it was only the second sister, who wept tears of joy to see him recovering. For her, too, it had been love at first sight!

That night the young couple lay snug in the straw and made plans for their future together as the sounds of battle faded farther and farther away. They talked of many silly things: babies and cottages and birds and nests, but not once did anyone mention buttons. No, not once.

"I shall write to Papa," said the girl in the morning. "A letter or something."

In the meantime, the youngest sister went every day to the meadow by the river and ran to and fro in the long grass, her apron held out before her.

She was her father's last hope, had he but known!

Running is good exercise, and soon his youngest daughter grew strong and sturdy, so she was not as unhappy as she might have been, for the truth is that not a single button fell into her apron. No, not even a cuff link. It was enough to discourage a saint, but still she got up every morning and did her best. For isn't it written somewhere that if at first you don't succeed, try, try again?

There is no telling how long she might have gone on, but one day a young cowherd who brought his beasts down to the water morning and night stopped to watch her. At first he was merely puzzled by her antics, but then he grew to love the way her brown legs flashed through the green grass.

He watched her every day for a week, and then on Sunday evening plucked up his courage and called to her as she cantered by.

"Pray, love, what are you doing, running back and forth like that with your skirts a-flying and your apron all billowy?"

The youngest sister was quite out of breath and so was glad to stop and talk for a minute. She told him of her task and how hard she was trying.

"And how many buttons have you got so far?" asked the young cowherd.

"Not one. Not even one of those cheap wooden ones off an old overcoat. I don't think there are any buttons up in the sky at all," she said, and sat down on a bank of crown vetch to cry a bit with her pretty brown feet stretched out before her.

"Don't cry, love," said the young cowherd. "Listen to me. Tomorrow morning, why don't you try running underneath that old oak tree in the center of the meadow? I understand there's a frequent fall of buttons there."

"Really?" said the youngest sister, hardly daring to hope.

"Really. Last week there was a veritable hailstorm of brass shirt studs. Right beneath the place where the leaves are thickest."

Well! He had such a way with words that the girl couldn't help but believe him.
So the next morning she did as he had told her and ran round and round under
the old oak. And what do you think?

Just as she ran under the thickest cluster of leaves, down fell a set of used trouser
buttons into her apron!

Who can describe the joy which greeted her when she returned home! Her mother sewed the buttons immediately onto her father's britches, and the old man capered about like a child, so glad he was to be out of bed once more.

And when their daughter told them of the young cowherd who had helped and advised her, what could they say? They said nothing would be too good for such a wise young man, which is exactly what the girl thought, too.

That evening, when he brought the beasts to water, there she was, sitting in the crown vetch with a chain of daisies around her head.

"Well, love, did you get your buttons?" he asked.

"Yes, I did, and all because of you. How can I ever repay you?" The poor girl was willing to give him everything she possessed, but even that, she said, couldn't possibly be enough.

"I don't know," said the cowherd. "Perhaps we should get married. For it is often said that between a husband and wife there can be no debts, but they must share all and all together."

"Yes. You must be right. We should get married at once," said the girl, and they kissed rapturously.

And here is a picture of their wedding party. There is the bride's father and mother. Doesn't he look proud with all his buttons done up? And look at that! The eldest sister has come back from Cologne for the occasion with her bargee husband. There they are with their new baby. Don't they look happy together? And there is the sister with the bold ensign! Aren't they a handsome couple? Why, they look strong enough to win a war all by themselves.

But of course no one is as beautiful as a bride. There she is. Right in the middle of the picture. And the clever cowherd? Well, he is very good-looking, too. That's him next to her, with his trousers tied up with a bit of string. He doesn't seem to have enough buttons, but she doesn't care. It's a small fault and seems to run in the family.